P9-AFZ-184

WITHDRAWN

Jimmy
the Greatest!

JAIRO BUITRAGO

Pictures by
RAFAEL YOCKTENG

Translated by Elisa Amado

Groundwood Books / House of Anansi Press
Toronto   Berkeley

In a town like Jimmy's there is usually only one small church and, if you're lucky, a little gym where you can hit a punching bag, skip rope or box.

Here's Jimmy. He's the guy with the shoes.

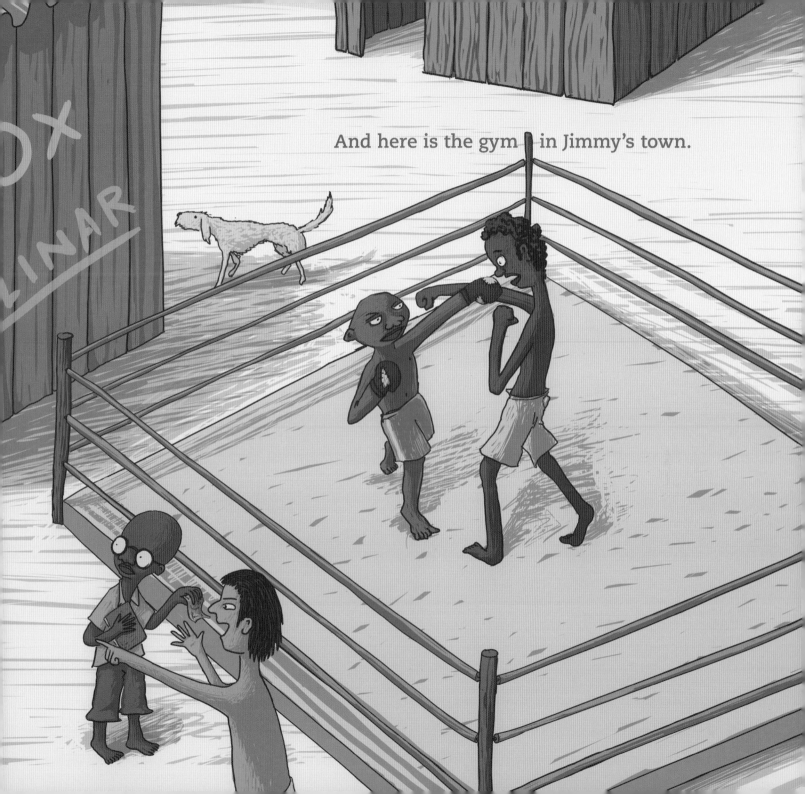

And here is the gym   in Jimmy's town.

Our story begins when Don Apolinar, the owner of the gym, looked at Jimmy properly for the first time and suggested he take a run around the town. Since Jimmy didn't have much else to do, he started training.

That very day Jimmy told his grandfather that he wanted to become a boxer, and he promised his mother that he'd buy her a new icebox when he did.

In his heart Jimmy was already a boxer, even though there were no boxing gloves at the gym, and someone there, maybe by mistake, had taken his shoes.

Don Apolinar gave Jimmy a cardboard box filled with books and newspaper clippings. There was also a note saying, "Muhammad Ali's bike was stolen when he was little."

But who was Muhammad Ali?

Jimmy read and re-read the books and clippings. He read as he never had before, using the glasses that he had never worn.

His mother
was surprised
to see Jimmy
reading and
shadow-
boxing at the
same time.

Jimmy
felt good.
He wasn't
sure why,
but he did.
He wasn't
thinking
about
what he
didn't have
anymore...
He didn't
need much
stuff to
run.

Nor to get others to follow along.

Hear me out.
My name is Jimmy.
I don't say much.
My fist is strong.
My words have clout.

From my eyes
the sun shines free.
If you take me on,
I'll knock you down.
Listen to me.
I'm a storm at sea.

I'm the champ.
Only last week,
I murdered a
rock,
injured a
stone,
hospitalized a
brick,
wrestled an
alligator
and got home
in time
to make lunch
for Gramps.

Jimmy loved to talk about strange things like respect and dignity, though people didn't always listen.

And even without any shoes, his future as a boxer was looking bright. Not many people dared to get in the ring with him.

BOX APOPULAR

But things change.
Don Apolinar, like many people in town, had to go to the big city — that faraway place where there are boxing matches, gyms and real jobs.

Jimmy was glad for Don Apolinar, though it wasn't easy to say goodbye to his trainer. Especially now that he realized how much he still had to learn.

Like how not to let time pass him by...

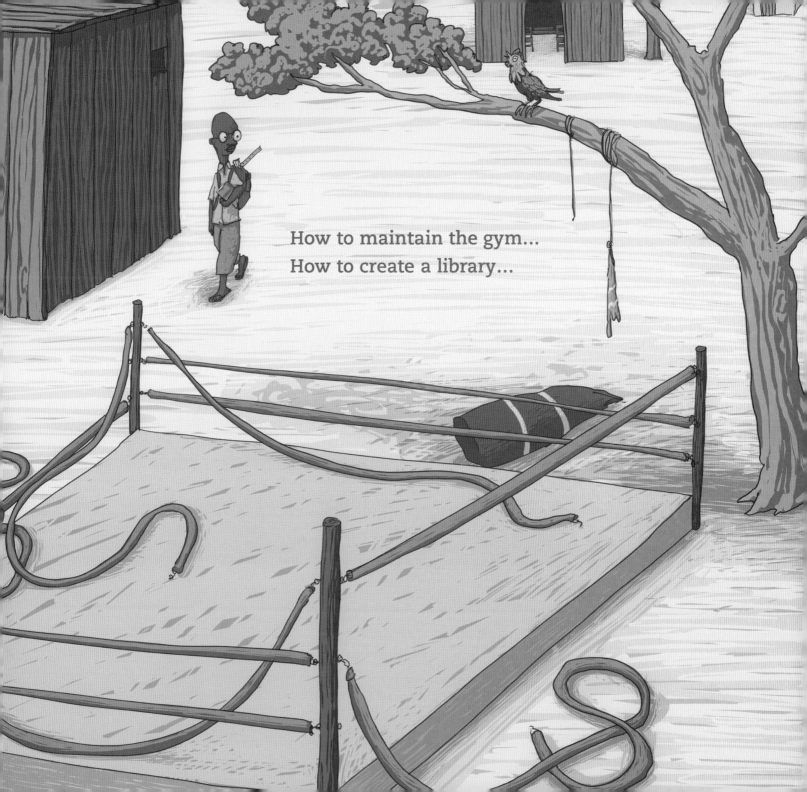

How to maintain the gym...
How to create a library...

Yes, in towns like Jimmy's people often leave to make a new life. But for now Jimmy is staying.

Maybe one day he'll get a match.

Listen to me.
This is my town.
There are donkeys, three sheep
and the great huge sea.
There are no elegant houses
or fancy things.
But we're really great.
We dance and we box
and we don't
sit around waiting
to go someplace else.

Goodbye, my story's over.
Remember my name.
Between the sky
and the sea,
there's me, Jimmy —
Jimmy the Greatest.

Text copyright © 2010 by Jairo Buitrago
Illustrations copyright © 2010 by Rafael Yockteng
English translation copyright © 2012 by Elisa Amado
First published in Spanish in 2010 by Random House
Mondadori, Bogotá, Colombia
First published in English in Canada and the USA in 2012 by
Groundwood Books
Third printing 2013

All rights reserved. No part of this publication may be
reproduced, stored in a retrieval system or transmitted, in
any form or by any means, without the prior written consent
of the publisher or a license from The Canadian Copyright
Licensing Agency (Access Copyright). For an Access
Copyright license, visit www.accesscopyright.ca or call toll
free to 1-800-893-5777.

Groundwood Books / House of Anansi Press
110 Spadina Avenue, Suite 801, Toronto, Ontario M5V 2K4
or c/o Publishers Group West
1700 Fourth Street, Berkeley, CA 94710

We acknowledge for their financial support of our
publishing program the Government of Canada through the
Canada Book Fund (CBF).

Library and Archives Canada Cataloguing in Publication
Buitrago, Jairo
Jimmy the greatest! / Jairo Buitrago ; Rafael Yockteng,
illustrator ; Elisa Amado, translator.
Translation of: ¡Jimmy, el más grande!
ISBN 978-1-55498-178-6
I. Yockteng, Rafael II. Amado, Elisa III. Title.
PZ7.B8857Ji 2012   j863'.7   C2011-906031-0

The illustrations were created digitally.
Design and art direction by Camila Cesarino Costa
Printed and bound in China

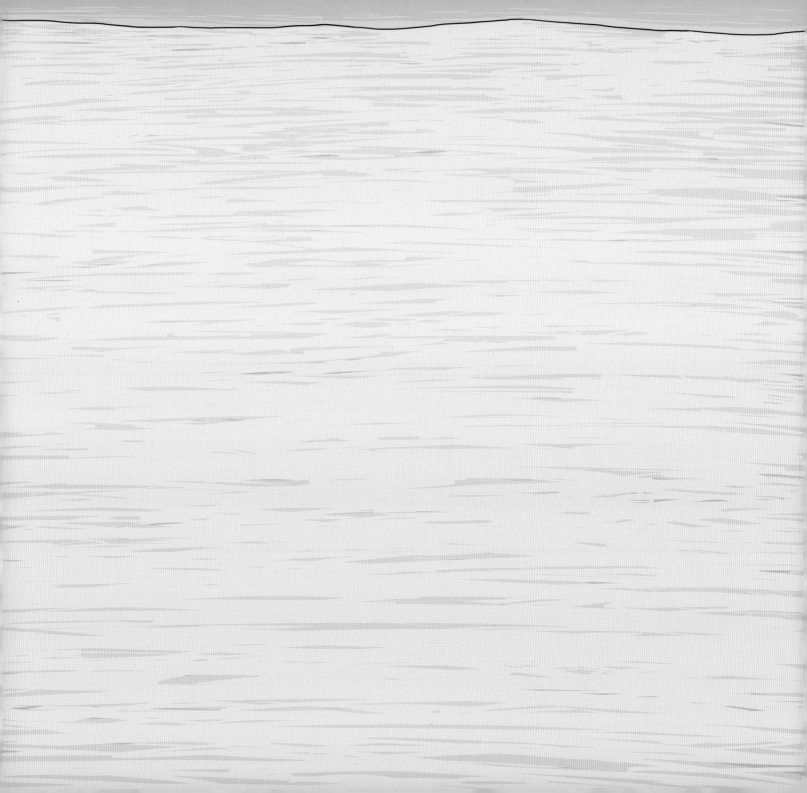

31901068171380